Jim Henson's™
SPLASH AND BUBBLES™

Shark Surprise

Based on the series created by John Tartaglia
Based on the TV series teleplay written by David Cain, Laura Sams, and Robert Sams
Adaptation by Liza Charlesworth

Houghton Mifflin Harcourt
Boston   New York

ISBN: 978-1-328-85275-5 paper over board
ISBN: 978-1-328-85280-9 paperback

hmhco.com

Printed in China
SCP 10 9 8 7 6 5 4 3 2 1
4500695631

It was a lovely afternoon in Reeftown. Dunk was taking a nice, long nap. He floated and bobbed along until . . .

"OUCH!" Dunk felt something poke him from the ocean floor. He floated up to take a look.

Dunk showed Splash and Bubbles the sharp white object.

"What is it?" asked Bubbles.

"It's a tooth!" answered Dunk.

"Let's find out who this mystery tooth belongs to!" said Splash.

The friends swam around, searching for clues. What did they find? Teeth! Lots and lots of teeth! What kind of fish loses teeth?

Sometimes old fish lose their teeth. So they went to see their old pal Gush.

"Sorry, kids," he said, "those aren't my teeth. But why don't you show them to Denny?"

Denny cleaned everyone's teeth in the whole reef. Surely she'd know who had lost them.

The kids found Denny working in Maury the eel's mouth.

"Do you know whose tooth this is?" asked Splash.

"Wow! You don't see many shark teeth around here," she said.

"Sh-sh-sh-shark!" exclaimed Dunk.

"Yes. A zebra bullhead shark, to be exact," Denny said. "There's one that lives in a cave on the edge of the reef."

A shark in Reeftown? A shark with missing teeth would be extra cranky! They needed to return the missing teeth pronto. Just then, someone new swam up. "Hey, I'm Zee," she said. "Nice to meet you!"

Zee seemed friendly. The kids explained that they were looking for a shark.

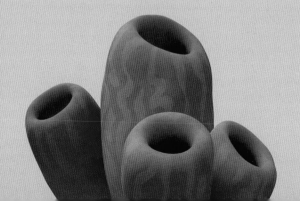

"Sharks are big and mean and scary," said Dunk.

"And they have lots of teeth," added Bubbles.

Zee opened her mouth. She had lots of teeth.

"And they have big dorsal fins," said Splash.

Zee turned and showed them her big dorsal fin.

Then Zee whirled around and shared a
shark fact of her own:
"Did you know sharks have five gill slits
like these?" she asked.

"Are you a shark expert too?" asked Dunk.

"I guess you could say that," said Zee, "seeing as how I'm a . . . SHARK!"

Splash, Bubbles, and Dunk laughed. Zee was way too small and friendly to be a shark.

"Will you help us find the shark?" asked Splash.

"If I go with you, you'll DEFINITELY find a shark," said Zee with a wink.

FIN FACT: There are more than 350 different kinds of sharks. They can be gray, white, tan, striped, and spotted, and even have heads shaped like hammers. Sharks come in all sizes, too. The smallest is as short as a pencil, and the largest is as long as a bus!

Zee and the kids found the cave
at the edge of the reef.
"This is where Denny said the shark
lives," said Bubbles.
"I happen to know for a fact that a shark
lives here," said Zee confidently.

The cave was dark and
creepy. The kids were
afraid to enter. But not Zee.
She swam right inside!

"Is there a shark in there?" called Bubbles.
"Yep, sure is," Zee shouted back.

They peeked inside the cave. Oh no! A shadowy shape was swimming closer and closer. It had a large dorsal fin. It looked big and mean and scary.

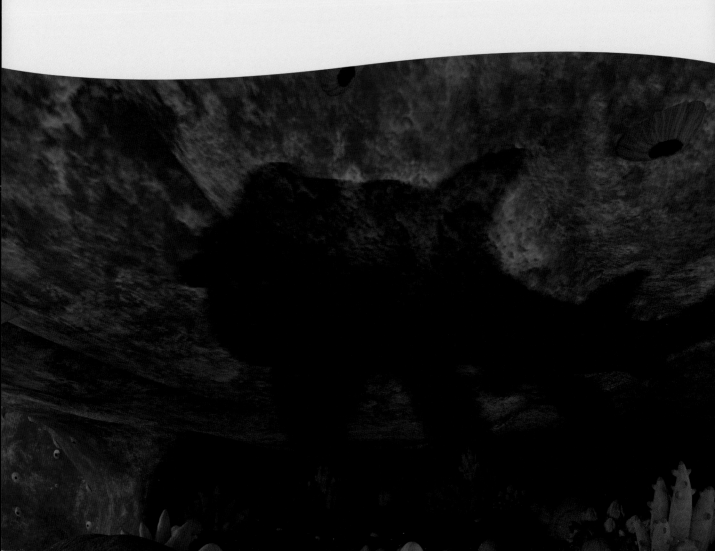

"SHARK!" shouted Splash.

"Please don't eat me!"
begged Dunk.

At last, the shape came out of the cave.
It was . . . Zee!

"Welcome to my home," she said.

The kids were shocked. Zee really WAS a shark!

"But you're so small!" Bubbles said. "I thought sharks were big and scary."

Zee grinned. "Sharks come in all shapes and sizes."

"But the teeth we found can't be yours, because you have all your teeth," said Dunk.

"Zebra bullhead sharks lose their teeth all the time," replied Zee. She spit out a tooth to prove it!

FIN FACT:
Sharks have lots and lots of teeth—as many as 3,000! Their teeth are arranged in rows. When one tooth is lost, another quickly takes its place.

"Do you want your lost teeth back?" asked Splash. But Zee said she didn't need them.

"I have a never-ending supply," she explained. "When one falls out, there's always another ready to replace it."

Then Zee opened wide to show off all her shiny
white shark teeth.

"Wow!" said Dunk. "Sharks really are amazing!"
Bubbles and Splash agreed.

Sharks truly did come in all shapes and sizes. Zee was small and striped and not scary at all.

"Oh, and did I mention that sharks are VERY fast swimmers?" said Zee.

"I think it's time for . . . Ocean Tag!" Splash said.
And their new friend Zee called, "You're it!"